I Want To Fly!

Written by Andre´ A. Lewis
Illustrated by Livio Ramondelli

3rd Printing

ISBN: 978-0-9791868-0-6

Library of Congress Control Number: 2006911264

Published by Abutech LLC
7948 Winchester Road Suite 109-257
Memphis, Tennessee 38125   USA

Printed in China by Everbest Printing Co.
through Four Colour Imports, Louisville, Kentucky   USA

To my three daughters -
Taylor, Sydney, and Reagan
Love, AAL

"I want to fly!" I say,
peering at wispy clouds in the pale blue sky.

Grandpa finishes sipping his morning coffee while standing on the porch. "Are you ready to go?" he says, as he fastens the last button on his old gray work overalls.
"Yes, sir, I'm ready," I say as I follow his footsteps.

"We'd better cross before the train comes," I say. Since his accident, Grandpa can't walk as fast, so I wait for him to cross the tracks.

"I used to ride the trains when I was a boy," Grandpa says, smiling underneath his favorite Cincinnati Reds baseball cap. He still loves to watch the games on his black-and-white TV.
"I like trains, but I want to fly an airplane," I say.

I enjoy spending the summer with my Grandpa. While Spot, their cat, saunters by, waving his tail, I hear a rooster singing, "Cock-a-doodle-doo".

Click-clack.

Bam-boom.

The man with the blue-and-white hat waves at us while he blows his horn. "Choo! Choo!"

As I run down the hill with my hands stretched wide,
I imagine floating into the air with blue
jays and cardinals.
"I can fly. I can fly. High into the sky."

Grandpa just smiles at me as he goes
to get the axe out of the shed.

"Come on, Miles, we've got to get
started now. I have twelve pork
shoulders to cook."

"Mmmm, Mmmm. You make the
best barbeque in the world,
Grandpa," I say.

It's my job to place the hickory on the chopping block. Then Grandpa takes his trusted axe and raises it into the air. With one swift blow, Grandpa splits the wood in two. "CRACK!"

Quietly, while Grandpa tends to the fire, I walk through the grassy path to my favorite place. My field of dreams is filled with huge cattails, standing high and bending in the gentle breeze. Bunches of blackberries and red berries are my treat to eat while I drink the sweet juice from the honeysuckles.

I lay back with my hands behind my head. I take off my shoes, so my toes can wiggle in the dirt. I take a blade of grass and place it in my mouth, like I saw in a book at school about a boy my age floating on a raft.

Looking at the clouds, I see so many things. I see a boat floating in the air, with its two big stacks bellowing clouds out of the top. "Sailing on a boat would be fun," I say.

Suddenly, an airplane whisks across the sky, leaving a trail of clouds behind. It seems so far away, because I can't hear it make a sound.

"Miles, come on and help me with the fire," Grandpa says.

I scramble to tie my shoes and brush the dirt off my clothes. Several cockleburs have nested in my short, black hair, and they prick my fingers as I take them out.

"I'm coming, Grandpa," I yell.

Spreading my arms out wide, I start my engine roaring. "Hum. Hum. Hum."
Then, like a rock out of a slingshot, I explode, running as fast as I can.

"I can do it. I can do it," I say, leaping into the air to soar above the ground.
I close my eyes and feel the gentle wind against my face.

I'm weightless, floating like
a bird. With the grace of a
swan, my feet finally touch
the ground again.

Grandpa, with sweat dripping from his brow, places the flat-edged shovel into the blazing fire.

"Boy, the fire is hot today." He takes the burning, red-hot hickory cubes and gingerly walks over to the pit.

"I've got it Grandpa," I say. I open the tin grate to the barbeque pit. I can feel the heat from the shovel as it passes by.

Grandpa lines the pit on both sides with the piping-hot wood. "That's enough now," he says. "It's time for a break."

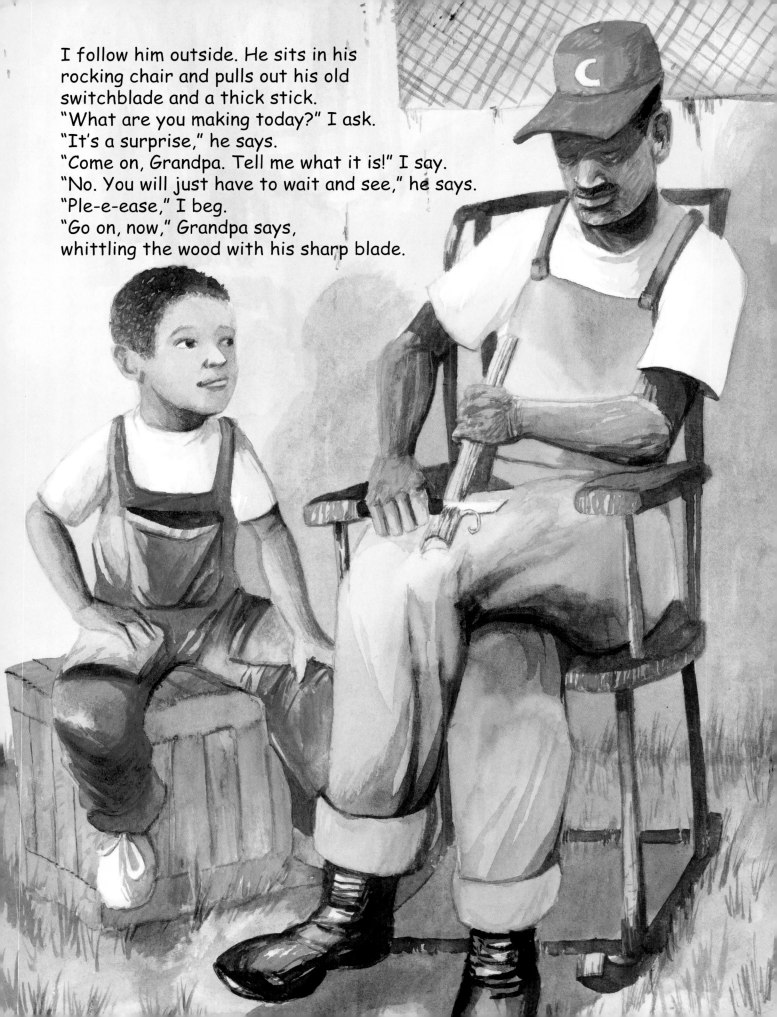

I follow him outside. He sits in his
rocking chair and pulls out his old
switchblade and a thick stick.
"What are you making today?" I ask.
"It's a surprise," he says.
"Come on, Grandpa. Tell me what it is!" I say.
"No. You will just have to wait and see," he says.
"Ple-e-ease," I beg.
"Go on, now," Grandpa says,
whittling the wood with his sharp blade.

Mr. Sam Lamar, the storeowner, walks out onto the porch. "How are we doing today?" he asks.
"We're doing just fine," Grandpa says.

Mr. Lamar looks over at me as I play in the front of the store with my arms still spread wide. "What's he doing there, Jimmy?"

"Miles wants to fly an airplane, Mr. Lamar."
"Oh really?" Mr. Lamar says, scratching his chin. "Has he ever been in a plane before?"
"No, sir. Don't think it bothers him. He thinks he can fly."

"Well, Jimmy, I think I can do something about that."

Mr. Lamar goes back into the store.

Grandpa takes the last shoulder off the barbeque grill. I play with my hands stretched out wide.

As Grandpa rocks in his chair, whittling away, a big, red truck drives up.

On the side of the door, there is a plane on it with some writing: "Big Red's Crop Dusting."
A tall, thin man steps out of the truck and walks into the store. I look at Grandpa, and he looks at me. Then Mr. Lamar and the tall man walk out onto the porch.

"Jimmy, this here is Mr. Jones," Mr. Lamar says.
"He dusts my crops every year."
"Nice to meet you, Mr. Jones," Grandpa says.
He shakes Grandpa's hand. "Nice to meet you, too," Mr. Jones says.
"Well, Jimmy? Sam tells me somebody around here wants to fly an airplane."

My eyes get wide as my heart
begins to beat faster and faster.
The man is looking at me with a
big grin.

"So, would you like to go fly in my
plane?" Mr. Jones asks.

I look at Grandpa and smile so
hard my face hurts.
I didn't even have to ask.
"Yes, you can go," Grandpa says.

I wrap my arms around his waist.
"Thanks, Grandpa!"

Mr. Jones, Grandpa, and I drive out to the country. Mr. Jones has a small landing strip and a beautiful red plane.

My insides are shaking as I get out of the truck.
"Come on, Miles, let's go," Mr. Jones says, picking me up
and placing me in the front seat. He straps me in tight
and gives me a pair of goggles. He climbs into the back.

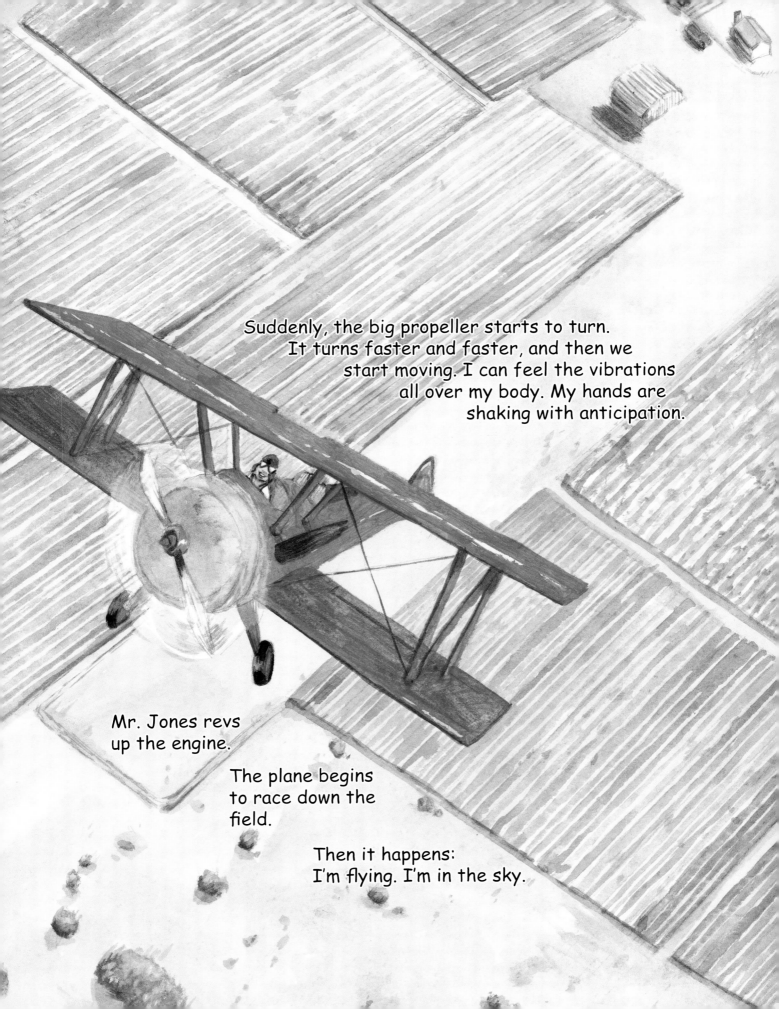

Suddenly, the big propeller starts to turn.
It turns faster and faster, and then we
start moving. I can feel the vibrations
all over my body. My hands are
shaking with anticipation.

Mr. Jones revs
up the engine.

The plane begins
to race down the
field.

Then it happens:
I'm flying. I'm in the sky.

Looking over the side, everything becomes smaller. I see cars that look like my play cars. I can almost reach out and touch the clouds with my hand.

"Miles, grab the stick," Mr. Jones says.
"What?" I scream.
"It's okay. Put your hands on the stick and follow me."
I hold onto the stick between my legs.
It goes left, and the plane turns left.
It goes right, and the plane turns right.

Mr. Jones takes the controls again, and we go back to the landing field. He points the airplane toward the ground. The trees become bigger. It looks like we are going into the cornfield. Then he pulls back on the stick, and we ease onto the ground. He stops the plane right by his red truck.

Mr. Jones gets out of the plane, and Grandpa walks our way. Mr. Jones takes me out, and I shake his hand.

"Thank you Mr. Jones for the plane ride!" I say.

"Miles, it was my pleasure," says Mr. Jones with a big smile. "Your Grandpa is waiting."

I turn and run into my Grandpa's arms.

"Grandpa, I was flying," I say.
"Yes, you were, Miles," Grandpa says as he puts me back down.
"I've got something."
He reaches into his pocket. He hands me the piece of wood he was whittling on. It is a set of wings with my name on it. They look like the wings pilots wore in those war movies on TV.
"Thank you, Grandpa. I love you," I say, holding the wings in my hand.

Mr. Jones takes us back to the store, and we walk up the hill and across the tracks. "Grandpa, I really flew an airplane today," I say, holding on to his hand, which is twice as big as mine.

"Miles, I always knew you could fly," he says, limping down the hill from the tracks to the house, with the sun setting behind us.